Disney's
The Further Adventures of
Aladdin
1 A Thief in the Night

BY A. R. Plumb

ILLUSTRATED BY
Laureen Burger
Mark Marderosian
H. R. Russell

DISNEP PRESS

NEW YORK

Library of Congress Catalog Card Number: 94-71483
ISBN: 0-7868-4016-1
FIRST EDITION
1 3 5 7 9 10 8 6 4 2

Disney's
The Further Adventures of

Aladdin

1 A Thief in the Night

"I'm sorry, Rajah," said Princess Jasmine. She stroked her pet tiger's head. "I know you want to go to the banquet tonight. But I'm afraid you might scare away the other guests. They won't understand that you're just a sweet little pussycat with very big teeth."

"If he's a pussycat, then I'm a chickadee," muttered Iago the parrot. He was perched on the Sultan's shoulder. Iago, the Sultan, and Jasmine were in the throne room waiting for Aladdin and Abu. "Come on, Your Majesty," said Iago, "let's get moving. I'm starving. I'm so hungry I could eat a camel!"

Before the Sultan could answer, Aladdin ran into the throne room. "Abu is missing!" he said breathlessly. "I can't find him any-where."

"Confound it! That monkey is such trouble," said the Sultan.

Jasmine tapped her foot. "We need to hurry, Aladdin. The dinner at Hassan's starts in half an hour." Hassan was a rich

merchant who had recently moved to Agrabah. He lived in a large house in the center of town. That evening he was giving a dinner party in honor of a famous sorcerer named Zoran.

"I can't leave without Abu," Aladdin said.

"But we mustn't be late," said the Sultan. "It wouldn't do. I am the ruler of Agrabah, after all. I should set a good example. All the guests will be waiting."

"Who else is coming, Father?" Jasmine asked.

"I'm not sure, dearest," the Sultan replied. "The invitation just said it would be a night to remember." He rubbed his stomach. "I wonder if they'll serve any poppyseed cake."

Jasmine reached for Aladdin's hand. "Don't worry," she said. "I'm sure Abu will turn up. He's probably with the Genie."

Suddenly the sound of hoofbeats filled the air. A moment later a zebra galloped into the throne room.

But this was no ordinary zebra. It was wearing a little fez and a vest.

Aladdin sighed. The Genie was always turning Abu into a variety of strange animals. "Abu?" Aladdin asked. "Is that you?"

The zebra nodded. He did not look very happy. In fact, he looked about as angry as a zebra in a vest could look.

The Genie appeared in the doorway in a puff of blue smoke. "What do you think?" he asked. "I'm decorating my rumpus room in stripes. I thought a zebra would add a nice touch." The Genie had been trapped in a magic lamp for ten thousand years until Aladdin had set him free. He still lived in his lamp, but now he could come and go when he pleased. The lamp made a very nice house, especially now that the Genie had started remodeling. He had already added a rumpus room and a sauna.

Iago flew over and perched on Abu's head. "Not bad," he said. "Much better than that mangy monkey fur."

"Genie," said Aladdin. "Could I please have my monkey back? We're going to be late for dinner."

The Genie tapped his chin. "Dinner? You're going to dinner? Will it be a black-tie affair, by any chance?" *Poof!* Suddenly the zebra was wearing a black-and-white checked bowtie.

"Whoopsie! That was supposed to be a *black* tie," the Genie said. "Ever since Al set me free, the old powers aren't quite what they used to be." He shook his head and gazed at the zebra. "Checks with stripes? Ugh!" *Zap!* The zebra's whole body was covered with checks. *Zap! Zap!* A set of checkers appeared. The Genie jumped a black checker across the zebra's back. "King me!" he cried. "Or should I say, *Sultan* me?"

"Genie," said Aladdin. "I'm serious. We're late. Fix Abu — please?"

The Genie shrugged. "Well, if you insist, Al. Back by popular demand. Ta-daa! It's

monkey boy!"

Zap! Abu turned back into his old monkey self. He shook his finger at the Genie. He chattered and grumbled. He scowled and stamped his feet.

"No need to thank me," said the Genie, patting Abu on the head.

"Now that Abu's himself again, we'd better go," said the Sultan. "We don't want to miss the first course, you know."

They headed out into the cool desert night. The Genie waved good-bye from the palace door. "Have fun, kids," he called. He zapped himself into a big blue furry dog. "And don't forget the doggy bag!"

A few minutes later the Sultan's carriage
pulled up in front of Hassan's grand house.

"You look wonderful," Aladdin said to
Jasmine as he helped her out of the
carriage.

"Thanks. So do you," she said.

Aladdin blushed. "I hope so. I guess I'm
a little nervous about tonight. I'm still not
used to these fancy dinners. I'm afraid I
won't know what to say to anyone."

"Don't worry," said Jasmine, squeezing
his hand. "You'll have plenty of interesting
stories to tell at dinner."

A servant opened the front door, and they entered a grand marble hallway. Richly colored carpets covered the walls and the floor, and gold and brass objects gleamed in the light of hundreds of candles. Hassan ran forward to greet his guests. He was a round man with a pointed beard and a very big grin.

"Your Majesty," the merchant cried. "It is my most extreme honor and glorious pleasure to welcome you to my humble home." He bent and kissed the Sultan's right hand. Then he frowned and pulled back. "But where is the Mystic Blue Diamond?" he asked.

"What? Oh, ah, it's here, on my other hand," said the Sultan. He held out his left hand so that the large blue stone of his ring sparkled in the light.

"What a relief! I was afraid you hadn't worn it," said Hassan.

"Afraid?" the Sultan asked.

"I meant . . . I meant that I've heard of

the Diamond's great power. And of course I've longed to see it for myself." He grabbed the Sultan's hand and gazed at the ring for a very long time.

"Er — could I please have my hand back?" the Sultan asked.

"A thousand pardons," Hassan said. He turned to Jasmine. "Ah, Princess Jasmine. What an honor. Everything I have heard is true. Your beauty is as blinding as the desert sun."

"Good line," Iago whispered to Aladdin. "You oughta write that down, loverboy."

Aladdin tried to poke Iago in the ribs. But Iago fluttered out of his reach just in time, and Aladdin lost his balance. He stumbled back against a tall vase on a pedestal.

The vase toppled and fell. Aladdin made a dive for it. He caught it just before it hit the floor.

"Oops," said Aladdin. He put the vase back. "Sorry."

Hassan stared at him for a moment through narrowed eyes. "Your Most Esteemed Majesty," he said to the Sultan, "your servant boy seems a little clumsy. Perhaps you would allow me to be so bold as to recommend a more surefooted replacement from my own staff."

Aladdin's face turned bright red. He couldn't believe it — even in his fancy clothes he was being mistaken for a lowly servant!

The Sultan just laughed. "Oh, Aladdin's not my servant, Hassan. Someday he's going to marry Jasmine and take over my kingdom."

Hassan's eyes widened. "I see. I apologize, young man, for my most regrettable ignorance. And I also apologize to you, Your Majesty, from the depths of my heart, which beats only that I may serve you. Please forgive me."

"Of course, of course," said the Sultan with a little wave. "Is dinner almost ready?"

"Indeed," said Hassan. "Follow me, if you please. Zoran the sorcerer is joyfully awaiting the pleasure of meeting you."

The dining hall glittered with silver and crystal. Servants ran to and fro, bringing in platter after platter of delicious-looking food. But almost all the chairs at the long table were empty.

"Where are all the other guests?" asked the Sultan.

Hassan gave him a mysterious smile. "This is a private affair, Your Highness," he said.

The Sultan, Aladdin, and Jasmine took their seats. Abu hopped onto the chair next to Aladdin's and eyed a tantalizing platter of sugared dates and figs.

"I've arranged seating for your little friends," said Hassan, grabbing Abu by the scruff of the neck. He pointed to two chairs at the far end of the long table. Books were piled on the seats.

"How flattering," Iago grumbled. "Booster seats. This Hassan guy is really turning out to be Mr. Tactful." He flapped over and sat down. Abu followed, after one last hungry glance at the dates. There was no food at all at this end of the table. Abu hoped the servants would bring some soon.

A very old man wearing a flowing black robe entered and bowed to the Sultan. He had a wispy white beard. His eyes were dark and wild. His pointed silver hat was tilted to one side.

"Sultan, allow me to introduce Zoran," said Hassan. "The most respected sorcerer in all the great wide desert."

14

"Can you do that rabbit-in-the-turban trick?" the Sultan asked eagerly. "I love that one."

"How about turning that ugly duckling into a beautiful swan, Your Majesty?" asked Zoran. He pointed a long silver wand at Iago.

Zap! Iago turned into an ostrich. Abu giggled and pointed.

Zoran blushed. "I'm afraid the old magic's starting to fade. He's supposed to be a swan."

"The Genie ought to meet Zoran," Aladdin whispered to Jasmine. "They have a lot in common."

"Hey, you! The whiz with the wand," Iago the ostrich grumbled. "Could I please have my body back?"

Zoran pointed his wand again. *Presto!* Iago turned back into a parrot.

"Wonderful, wonderful!" said the Sultan, chuckling and clapping his hands.

Zoran gave a modest bow. "A small enchantment, nothing more." He held up his wand. "I'd be nothing without this," he said. "It's been in my family for years."

"Just like the Sultan's Mystic Blue Diamond," Hassan said. He turned to the Sultan. "Please, Your Highness, tell us more about the ring's powers. The tales we hear about it are quite fantastic. I doubt they can be true."

"If you want to hear a tale about the Mystic Blue Diamond, you should ask Aladdin," the Sultan said. "He can tell you a good one." He eyed a servant who was approaching with a large silver platter filled with lentil patties. He had a feeling he was going to be too busy eating to want to tell any stories for a while.

Hassan turned to Aladdin. "Do share the story with us, if you please, young man."

This was Aladdin's chance to show Hassan how wrong he'd been to mistake him for a servant. He knew he shouldn't brag — at least that's what Jasmine was always telling him. Still, he couldn't resist the chance to show off just a little. . . .

"I can tell you plenty, Hassan," said Aladdin.

"It all began back when I was still a street rat," Aladdin said as the food was served. "At least that's what the merchants in the marketplace called me. But I had dreams — big dreams." He gave Hassan a smile. "I'm sure you've heard of a man named Jafar. He was the Sultan's most trusted adviser. And Iago's old friend."

"Acquaintance," Iago corrected. "I hardly knew the guy, really."

"The trouble started when Jafar decided he wanted to rule Agrabah," Aladdin continued. "The Mystic Blue Diamond was one of the things he needed because of its incredible magic powers. But in the end, Jasmine and Abu and I were able to outwit Jafar and save the kingdom." He went on to tell Hassan and Zoran the whole story, including how he had tricked Jafar into wishing to become a genie so he would be trapped inside his new lamp.

"We thought it was all over then," Jasmine said. "But it wasn't."

"Yes, unfortunately, we weren't completely finished with Jafar," Aladdin said. "Not long after that he returned, more powerful than ever — and determined to get his revenge on me."

"Only *someone* saved the day," Iago said. "Not that I'm mentioning any names."

Aladdin rolled his eyes. "Yes, Iago did save the day."

"Of course, first he *helped* Jafar," Jasmine pointed out.

"But *then* I saved the day," Iago said.

"Afterward the Sultan asked me to be his

royal adviser," Aladdin said. "But I decided I wasn't ready for that yet. Too many meetings and rules."

"And you and the princess are planning to marry?" Hassan said.

"Aladdin and I decided to wait before we get married," Jasmine said. "We want to see the world and have adventures first." She smiled at Aladdin. "Lots of them."

"An impressive tale," said Hassan. He peered at the Sultan's shimmering ring. "There are men who would do anything to own such a gem as that, Sultan. No wonder you are so grateful to Aladdin."

"Yes, he's a fine boy," the Sultan said. "Pass the lentils, please."

Iago glanced at his empty plate and leaned close to Abu. "Something seems to be missing," he said. "Like food. Everyone else is already eating. What do we get? Table scraps?"

Abu peered down the long table at the food the others were eating. He wouldn't

mind eating scraps from *this* table. The variety was incredible. He couldn't wait to try every dish.

The Sultan wiped his mouth. "Will there be any poppy-seed cake for dessert, by any chance?" he asked Hassan.

"But of course," Hassan replied. He shared a smile with Zoran. "Poppy-seed cake like none you have ever tasted, Your Highness."

Finally a servant entered with two silver dishes for Abu and Iago. "I had the cooks make something special for you two," Hassan called to them.

Abu eagerly reached for his plate. Then he saw that it was filled with peanuts. He frowned. Peanuts were all right. But they were nothing compared with sugared dates, and lentil patties, and poppy-seed cake. . . .

Meanwhile, Iago stared down at his plate with disgust. It was filled with crackers. Iago hated crackers. There was only one thing he hated more than crackers — and that was people who fed him crackers. "I

knew I should have stayed home," he grumbled.

While everyone else was busy talking, Iago grabbed Abu and dragged the surprised monkey out of the room. He led him down a long hallway. Soon they reached a huge kitchen. Spicy smells filled the air. Food was piled high on every table and countertop. Abu's eyes nearly bugged out of his head as he looked around.

"This is more like it," Iago said. "Food everywhere! Where to start, where to start?"

Abu knew. He hopped onto a counter, grabbed a poppy-seed cake, and opened his mouth to take a bite.

"Hey, banana breath, didn't your mother teach you about sharing?" Iago yanked the whole cake away from Abu. "Feed me crackers, will you, Hassan?" Iago muttered. He stuffed a wingful of cake into his beak. "You know, there's something slimy about that guy and his sorcerer buddy. And nobody knows slimy better than me. I come from a long line of slime."

Iago gobbled up the last bit of the cake and licked his feathers. Abu scowled. That bird needed to be taught a lesson.

Abu spied a jar of hot curry powder. Perfect. He grabbed a lemon cake from the counter and made a hole in the top. Then he emptied the jar of curry powder into the hole and carefully covered it with frosting.

Abu scampered over to Iago and tapped him on the shoulder. Iago's beak was covered with frosting. Abu held out the cake with a big smile.

"What kind of chump do you think I am, chimp?" Iago demanded. "You think I was born in a birdcage? I know you stuck something in that cake."

Suddenly they heard voices at the other end of the kitchen. "Uh-oh! Bad news! It's Hassan and that sorcerer," Iago hissed. "Keep quiet." He ducked under a nearby table. Abu dropped the lemon cake and followed.

"You were right, Hassan," said Zoran. He was talking in a hushed voice. "That Sultan is an old fool. It will be easy to steal the Mystic Blue Diamond. And with it, my powers will be great indeed! Our plan cannot fail!"

"I think you mean *my* plan, Zoran." Hassan rubbed his hands together. "Once we have the Diamond, we will rule the land. With my brains and your wand, no one will be able to stop us!"

"What about *my* brains?" asked Zoran.

Hassan just smiled an evil smile. "Are you absolutely sure that sleeping potion is going to work?"

"Of course it will," said Zoran. "It's a piece of cake." He giggled. "Get it? We're putting the sleeping potion in the Sultan's slice of poppy-seed cake — so it's a *piece of cake!* Hee-hee!"

Hassan grabbed Zoran by the beard. "Forget the jokes, old man. Just tell me the potion will work," he growled.

"Well, if the Sultan starts to look woolly, we'll know I got it wrong," Zoran replied. "See, I store the *sleep*ing potion right next to the *sheep*ing potion."

Hassan let go of Zoran's beard. "You'd better hope you got it right. Before this night is over, I plan to be the ruler of all Agrabah. And nobody is going to stop me!"

As soon as Hassan and Zoran were gone, Abu dashed out of the kitchen. He had to warn Aladdin about the plot to steal the Mystic Blue Diamond. And there was no time to lose!

Iago flew down the hall after Abu. "Wait a minute, wait just a cotton-picking minute!" Iago called. "You can't just go rushing in there! That sorcerer guy will zap you into fried monkey. We need to sit back and think about this for a minute. Formulate a plan. Strategize."

Abu ignored him. In the dining hall,

servants were placing large slices of poppy-seed cake before the guests. Abu ran over and tugged hard on Aladdin's sleeve.

"There you are, Abu," Aladdin said. "It's almost time for dessert." He lowered his voice. "Don't worry about the peanuts, little buddy. I'll save you some cake."

Then Aladdin turned back to the others. They were all laughing and talking as if Abu weren't even there. Aladdin started telling a humorous story about a runaway camel.

Abu pulled on Aladdin's arm as hard as he could. He pointed at Hassan. He pointed at Zoran. Then he pointed at the Sultan and ran a finger across his throat.

But Aladdin still wasn't interested. "Abu, stop interrupting. I'm just getting to the funniest part of the story."

Iago stood in the doorway, watching Abu. He wondered if he should help him out. It could be dangerous — after all, Zoran was a sorcerer. But they had to warn the others, and it was clear that Abu wasn't getting anywhere with Aladdin.

Iago flapped over to where Abu was still pawing desperately at Aladdin. "Step aside and let a pro show you how it's done," he whispered to the monkey.

Iago landed on the table and walked over to Jasmine. "Hey, Princess," he muttered. "I've got the inside scoop on Hassan. And it ain't pretty."

Jasmine patted Iago's head absentmindedly. She was listening to Aladdin's story. "Shh," she said to Iago, putting a finger to her lips.

Just then she and the others burst out laughing at something Aladdin had said. Iago rolled his eyes. "Princess, you gotta believe me here," he said. He cleared his throat. "Princess, you gotta *listen* to me here! Yoo-hoo, Princess! Anybody home?"

Abu tugged on Iago's wing and pointed to the Sultan.

"You want me to tell the Sultan?" Iago asked. "I guess I could try. But the guy's got a few pieces missing from the old jigsaw puzzle, if you know what I mean."

Iago and Abu ducked under the table and hurried over to the Sultan. Abu pulled on his ankle. The Sultan didn't respond. Abu lifted the tablecloth and looked up. The Sultan was asleep! He was snoring softly. His napkin was on his belly. His turban was tilted. He looked very happy, and very full.

Iago angrily kicked the Sultan in the foot. "I can't believe it," he said. "The old guy ate so much he's out cold. Fast asleep. What are we going to do now? We're doomed. Dead meat!"

Suddenly Abu had a wonderful idea. Maybe they couldn't warn Aladdin and Jasmine about the plan to steal the Diamond. But maybe *they* could steal it before Hassan and Zoran did!

Abu grabbed Iago by a tail feather as the parrot was about to take off. "Hey, watch the merchandise," said Iago.

Abu pointed to the Sultan's left hand, which was dangling over the side of his chair. The Mystic Blue Diamond glittered in the candlelight.

Iago glanced from Abu to the ring and then back again. "*We* steal the ring before *they* steal the ring?" asked Iago. "Hey, I like your style! Not bad for a primate."

Iago grabbed the Sultan's ring and pulled. Abu shoved him aside. How typi-

cal — Iago was going to try to take credit for Abu's idea.

Abu tugged at the ring. It wouldn't budge.

"Move over, weakling," said Iago. He grabbed the Diamond with both wings and yanked with all his might.

The Sultan slipped under the table with a loud thud.

Abu and Iago heard a gasp. "Aladdin!" Jasmine cried. "Where's Father?"

Abu pushed Iago aside and gave a final yank. The ring came free. The Sultan kept snoring. Abu held up the shimmering Diamond in triumph. He loved jewels. He slipped the ring onto his finger.

"Give me that! Hand it over, you no-good furball!" Iago cried.

Abu shook his head. He wanted Aladdin to see how he'd saved the day. Besides, the ring looked very nice on him.

Aladdin and Jasmine peered under the table. "Abu! Iago!" Aladdin cried. "What are you two up to?"

Jasmine gasped. "He's got Father's Diamond!"

Abu leaped onto the table and held up the ring with a proud smile.

"The Diamond!" Hassan screamed. "That miserable monkey has the Mystic Blue Diamond!"

Under the table the Sultan stirred for a moment. "Is there any more cake?" he asked. Then he began to snore.

"Abu!" Aladdin cried. "Put that ring down!"

Abu scampered along the table, spilling drinks and leaving paw prints in the lentils.

"You'll have to forgive Abu," Aladdin said to Hassan. "He loves jewels." He gave the monkey a stern look. "Even when they happen to belong to somebody else."

"Give me that ring," Iago yelled. He flapped after Abu. "It was *my* idea to steal it, you oversize rat!" He grabbed Abu's tail. Abu shook it back and forth. Iago crashed into a bowl of fruit. The bowl tipped over, and the fruit went flying. A bright red apple hit Hassan right in the nose.

"Iago!" Jasmine cried. "Don't be rude to your host!"

"Rude?" Iago screeched. He was still holding on to Abu's thrashing tail. "RUDE? I'll give you rude. Your host is planning a heist! A diamond heist! He wants to rip off the ring! His pal with the defective wand is in on it, too. We stole the Diamond so they couldn't. It was all my idea."

The others gasped. "The bird is mad!" Hassan cried.

Jasmine knelt down next to the Sultan. "Aladdin!" she said. "Father won't wake up!"

"No kidding, kid," said Iago. "That's because they put sleeping potion in his cake."

"That's preposterous!" said Hassan.

But Aladdin had a hunch that Abu and Iago were telling the truth. He had to think fast. "Abu, throw me the Diamond," he called out.

Abu turned. He started to toss the ring. But just as he did, Iago finally let go of his tail. Abu lost his balance. He went flying — and so did the Diamond.

Abu landed headfirst in a kettle of fish soup. The Diamond landed in Hassan's soup bowl.

Abu peered out of the kettle. He had a fish under his fez.

"Oh, wonderful," said Iago. "Like the little ape didn't smell bad enough already."

Aladdin leaped forward and reached for the Diamond. But Hassan was faster. He scooped the ring out of his bowl. "Sorry,

street rat," Hassan hissed. "The Mystic Blue Diamond is mine."

"*Ours,* he means," said Zoran.

"The power of the Diamond will increase the power of Zoran's wand a thousand-fold," Hassan cried. "With both the wand and the Diamond, I will rule Agrabah forever!"

"*We,* he means," Zoran corrected. "*We'll* rule Agrabah forever."

"You thief! You can't do this," Jasmine cried angrily.

"And who is going to stop us?" asked Hassan. "One wrong move and I'll put your father to sleep — permanently." Hassan admired the ring on his finger. "Now give me the wand, Zoran."

Zoran hesitated. "But it's *mine.*"

Hassan stepped closer. "Give it to me, Zoran."

"But you don't know how to operate it! It takes years of training."

Hassan lurched for the wand and grabbed

it. He touched it to the ring on his finger. Suddenly the wand began to glow. It pulsed with light — purple, red, green, gold. Sparks shimmered from the Mystic Blue Diamond.

"See how powerful the wand is now?" Hassan cried as he waved it over his head.

Zoran looked lost without his wand. He shuffled toward the door. "Well, I guess we should be getting on to the palace, Hassan. Do you think I could sit on the throne first?"

Hassan's eyes glittered. "The palace! You think you're going to the palace? Why do I need you anymore, you wilted old wizard?" He pointed the glowing wand at the sorcerer. "I think it's time to try my first spell."

Iago could tell it was a good time to leave. "I'd love to stay for dessert, but it's getting late," he murmured. He backed through a nearby door into the hallway.

"But you promised me I could have my own throne," Zoran cried.

"You're a fool, old man. Can't you see I've made a monkey out of you?" Hassan smiled. "Come to think of it, that's a great idea!"

He pointed the wand at Zoran. The old sorcerer vanished in a cloud of silver smoke. In his place was a little monkey who looked just like Abu — fez and all. "Now, for the rest of you!" Hassan cried.

"Don't do it!" Aladdin shouted. Together he and Jasmine lunged for Hassan.

But it was too late. Hassan waved the wand again. The dining hall filled with thick smoke. Thunder boomed. Lightning flashed.

When the smoke cleared, two little Abus were standing in front of Hassan. Another was snoozing soundly where the Sultan had been a moment earlier. And one more was still sitting in the kettle of fish, looking confused.

Hassan cackled with pleasure. "Well, I'm off to take over Agrabah!" With a last evil laugh, he dashed away.

Just then Iago peered around the corner. His eyes went wide. Everywhere he looked he saw Abu.

"Oh no! It's my worst nightmare!" Iago shrieked. "Multiple monkeys!"

"Do something, Iago!"

Iago looked down. Aladdin's voice was coming out of one of the monkeys.

"Hurry, Iago!" said another monkey. This time it was Jasmine's voice. "If you hurry, you can fly after Hassan and catch him!"

"Catch him — are you crazy?" Iago asked. "Why would I want to do that? That guy is wacko. A real nutcase. Totally bonkers."

The real Abu gave Iago a grin. He held

up four fingers and pointed to Aladdin, Jasmine, and the Sultan.

"I see your point," Iago told Abu. "I can't handle this many monkeys in my life. Maybe I'd better see what I can do about that wacky thief."

He flew outside into the cool night air. In the distance he could see Hassan heading through the darkened marketplace toward the palace. "Ah, there we go," Iago muttered. "A thief in the night."

He caught up to Hassan quickly. Iago cleared his throat. In a perfect imitation of Zoran's voice, he spoke directly into Hassan's ear. "Stop right now, Hassan, or I'll turn you into an ostrich!" he shouted.

"Aaaaah!" Hassan screeched. He was so surprised he dropped Zoran's wand onto the sand. He stared around wildly, looking for the source of the voice.

"Serve *me* crackers, will you?" Iago said. He dove down and grabbed the wand. Then he flew back to Hassan's house.

"The wand!" Aladdin cried when he saw Iago. "Good work, Iago. But couldn't you get the Diamond, too? The wand isn't nearly as powerful by itself."

Iago rolled his eyes. "Oh, you're too kind," he said sarcastically. "I didn't mind at all, flying after Hassan and risking my neck for you. Please, don't try to thank me! I hate it when people make a fuss!"

"Just change us back, Iago, please?" said Jasmine. "We have to catch Hassan and get the Diamond. Tell him how to work the wand, Zoran."

Zoran scampered over. "Well, like you said, without the Diamond it's not as powerful. You'll have to imagine us the way we were before. Then point. And cross your fingers."

Iago pointed the wand at the group. He tried to imagine them as people again.

Buzz! Thwack! Zap! The room filled with smoke. Iago closed his eyes. When he opened them he saw the faces of Aladdin, Jasmine, and the others.

Unfortunately, that's all he'd changed.
They still had their monkey bodies.

"Try again, Iago," Jasmine said.

Iago closed his eyes. He tried to imagine
the rest of them.

Buzz! Thwack! Zap!

This time he got it right. Aladdin, Jasmine, the Sultan, and Zoran were back to
their old selves.

Jasmine straightened her robes. "Where was Hassan when you saw him, Iago?" she asked.

"The marketplace," said Iago. "I think he was lost — he was about to wander into the Thieves' Quarter."

"Uh-oh," said Aladdin. "We'd better hurry. If Hassan runs into the wrong person there, he may have his stolen property stolen from him!"

"Hey, Iago, can you *imagine* Zoran tied up?" Jasmine asked.

"You bet I can." Iago pointed the wand. In a flash, Zoran was neatly tied up. "You know, I could really get used to this kind of power."

"I'll take that," Jasmine said, grabbing the wand. "Keep an eye on Father, Iago. You help him, Abu." She looked over at the Sultan fondly. He was still snoring away.

Aladdin turned to Jasmine. "Well, we said we wanted adventure," he commented.

Jasmine rolled her eyes. "Come on," she said. "We don't have any time to lose."

The Thieves' Quarter was a dark and frightening place, especially at night. Scoundrels and criminals lurked in every corner. The black alleys and shadowy passageways had so many twists and turns that it was possible to get so lost one could never find the way out again. It was a place Aladdin knew well.

"Look!" Jasmine whispered. "Up ahead. It's Hassan."

"Stay here," said Aladdin. "I'll sneak around behind him. That way we'll have him cornered."

Aladdin ran through an alley and jumped

over a fence. He climbed up a rotting stair-
way to the top of an abandoned building.
When he got to the roof, he looked down.

Jasmine waved. She was waiting for his
signal.

Hassan was wandering down the narrow
street, looking lost. Every few seconds he
stopped and glanced around uncertainly.

"Hassan!" Aladdin cried. "You might as
well give up. You're surrounded."

"That's right," Jasmine said, stepping out
of the shadows.

Hassan looked up to the roof. "B-b-but
how? I turned you into monkeys!"

Aladdin held up the wand. "Iago
changed us back. We've already captured
Zoran."

"Well, you won't capture me, street rat!"
Hassan cried. He started to run.

Aladdin swallowed hard. It was a long
way down. But he didn't have much choice.
He aimed for Hassan and leaped off the
roof.

But Hassan was too quick. He dodged away in the nick of time. Then he vanished down a dark alley, heading toward the edge of town. "This way!" Aladdin called. "I know a shortcut." Jasmine dashed after him.

A few minutes later they found Hassan on the edge of town. The vast desert stretched out before them like a sandy sea. "Look!" Aladdin whispered. "Hassan's only a few steps from the Sands of Doom."

"The Sands of Doom?" Jasmine repeated.

"Quicksand," Aladdin explained. "Hassan will be swallowed up if he makes one wrong move. Oh yeah — be careful where you step."

"Hassan!" Jasmine called. "Give yourself up. Don't go any farther. My father will be merciful to you."

Hassan spun around. "You two again!" he cried. He held up the ring threateningly. "Don't come a step closer! Can't you see it's no good following me? With this ring I'm the most powerful person in Agrabah!"

Aladdin looked at the ring nervously.

But Jasmine was shaking her head. "He doesn't know how the Diamond works," she whispered to Aladdin. "Its energy gives power to other magic. But it can't perform magic by itself."

"Well, we'd better get it away from him before he figures that out," Aladdin whispered back.

"What are you two whispering about?" Hassan demanded.

"Oh, uh — I was just saying, maybe you're right, Hassan," Aladdin said. He grabbed the wand out of Jasmine's hand, giving her a secret wink. "You've got the Mystic Blue Diamond. I've got Zoran's wand. Suppose we put them together?"

Hassan threw back his head and laughed. "Me, band together with a mere boy — and a former street rat at that?"

"I could be useful to you," Aladdin pointed out. "I know all the tricks of the street. Besides, the ring and the wand are much more powerful together than apart. You said so yourself."

Jasmine stared at Aladdin, wide-eyed. "I hope you know what you're doing," she whispered.

"Hmm," Hassan said, staring at the wand in Aladdin's hand. "Perhaps you're right, dear boy. I may have spoken too hastily. Toss me the wand."

Aladdin nodded and threw the wand. It flew past Hassan and landed several yards out in the desert sand. "Oops," he said. "Sorry about that."

"Don't be silly, dear boy," said Hassan. "It is nothing."

Aladdin and Jasmine watched as Hassan dashed after the wand. Just as his fingers touched it, there was a horrible sucking sound. The wand began to sink into the sand—and so did Hassan's feet. His face

froze in terror. "Quicksand!" he cried. He held up the ring, obviously trying to free himself by magic, but nothing happened. He just kept sinking deeper and deeper. Soon he was waist deep. "You must help me!"

"Throw me the Diamond," said Jasmine.

"Never!" Hassan cried.

"See you around, then," said Aladdin.

"And thanks for the lovely dinner," Jasmine added.

Hassan's eyes were black with fear. He was up to his armpits in sand. "If I give you back the ring, how do I know you'll help me?" he cried.

"Don't you trust me?" asked Aladdin with a smile. "I'm a nice reliable guy, you know."

"All right then!" Hassan pulled off the ring and tossed it. It landed at Jasmine's feet. "Now help me!"

Aladdin looked at Jasmine. "Now what?"

"Now we save him," Jasmine said, picking up the ring.

Aladdin shrugged and grinned sheepishly. "How?"

"I thought you knew how," Jasmine cried.

"I didn't think that far ahead," Aladdin admitted.

"Oh, Aladdin!" Jasmine thought for a second, then snatched the sash from her waist. "We'll have to use this. I hope it will be strong enough."

"A homemade rope," Aladdin said. "Good idea." He tossed one end to Hassan.

Hassan stretched out his hand. After three tries he managed to grab the sash.

Jasmine and Aladdin grasped the other end tightly. Together they pulled and pulled.

With a loud sucking sound, Hassan came free. Slowly they dragged him to safety.

"Come on, Hassan," said Jasmine, clutching the Sultan's ring. "It's time to pay a little visit to Rasoul, the head of the palace guard." She smiled at Aladdin. "Then we can go wake up Father and return his ring!"

The stars were fading by the time everyone returned to the palace. They found the Genie and the magic carpet playing checkers in the throne room.

"Al, my man!" the Genie cried. "How was din-din?"

Aladdin laughed. "We almost bit off more than we could chew," he said, glancing at Jasmine. "But everyone got their 'just desserts' in the end."

The Sultan yawned. "I'm afraid I dozed off and missed all the excitement," he said.

Carpet jumped a checker across the board.

"I can't believe it!" the Genie cried. "This overgrown bath mat beats me every time!"

"This will make you feel better, Genie," said Jasmine. "Look what I brought you. When we went back to Hassan's to get Father, I took this wonderful lemon cake from the kitchen. I figured since Hassan interrupted our meal, he still owed us dessert."

"Interrupted?" asked the Genie.

"Long story," said Aladdin. "I'll tell you later."

Abu yanked on Jasmine's sleeve. He recognized that lemon cake. It was the lemon cake he'd made for Iago — the one with the hot curry powder in it.

Poof! The Genie zapped up a fork. A red napkin appeared around his neck.

Abu gulped. He looked at Iago.

Iago grinned back. "Dig in!" he said to the Genie.

The Genie took a big bite — a very big bite.

His blue face turned red. His hair sizzled and smoked. He began to expand, like a giant blue balloon. Then he opened his mouth. A long plume of flame came out.

"Three-alarm fire!" the Genie gasped. He clutched at his throat. "Call nine-one-one!"

Abu tried to creep away. Iago stepped on his tail.

"The monkey did it," Iago announced.

Abu closed his eyes.

He had the feeling he was about to be turned into another very interesting animal.